I0623190

Gourd Enough To Eat

Steamy Mountain Man Romance

Alphas Fall Hard

Sofia Aves

Blurb

She should never have walked into my shop, or up my mountain. But now Cadance Webster is here, she can work for her keep, even if it means breaking a few nails in the process.

This wilderness keeps secrets for all of us, and Cadance is no exception. Hell, I might even let her in if I didn't think she wasn't carrying a few of her own truths that could tear my whole world apart. Ones she's running from, all the way right into the mountains and into my arms.
And I'll be d*mned if she isn't a temptation gourd enough to eat.

First Edition

EBOOK ISBN 978-1-923471-88-7

PRINT ISBN 978-1-923471-13-9

CHAPTER ONE

ELIJAH

I stared at the pink glitter monstrosity of a van that marred the Lone Grizzly Mountain the Off-Duty Rescue Ranch sat on with my mouth open, catching flies. Hands that ached with hours of work wrangling a new horse that just wouldn't stay put forgot to hurt as I decoded the nude oversized animal decal one side.

A *Grin and Bear It* slogan decorated the front. I gazed at the pun, the naked bear—ha, the bare bear—all I could see. The eyesore obscured everything I loved about the ranch and the landscape, right up until a blonde bombshell of a girl hopped out of the driver's side. She was also covered in glitter and pink, fluffy stuff as she skipped around the front to chat with Ash, who ran the place.

He gave her a hug, his arms fitting around her where she had curves in all the right places. More than a few, actually. Hell, I didn't know jeans could look like that.

"She could rival you for a pun, gourd boy." Anson, one of the ranch's other workers, slapped my shoulder then cuffed at my face in play. "Fuck, man. You're drooling."

I jerked back with an oath. "Keep your hands to yourself," I grumbled.

Part of me wanted to watch her all day. The other part kind of admired her balls to stick a bear that big all over the front of her display—even if her display was a glitter van that looked like a pink version of the Mystery Machine, circa two thousand and one.

I swiped the back of my hand across my mouth just to check. He was right, dammit. That irked me worse than before. I turned my back on the glitter bomb and the girl who made a mess in the yard adjacent to the house, focusing on the rescue in front of us. "We have work to do," I snapped, succeeding only in frightening the creature, and probably Anson too, from the look on the man's face.

He turned away from the calamity in the making before me, grumbling like I had before. The sparkly new shiny thing in the yard might look like the best new distraction to come in from town, but I knew better.

Nothing good came from something so pretty. Anson could take my word for it, though right now he didn't seem inclined to ask, and I sure as hell wasn't about to offer my philosophy on life.

Today's newly arrived rescue horse, Daisy Duke, nuzzled my hand affectionately.

"Wanna feed, pretty girl?" I murmured, running my hand over her nose with extreme care, all too aware of the trust she put in me, offering me that first touch. Deep scars cut into her stunning chestnut coat around her head where she'd been trapped into a halter for an extended period by a previous owner who thought they were doing the right thing but...

Yeah, well. Sometimes owners did the wrong thing even when they thought they were doing the right thing. I was just glad that my job didn't involve talking to said owners. I figured my words would be too harsh for that end of a really blunt stick. Dusty, the local vet, lanced a pocket in her cheek earlier that looked like it was just swelling, and nothing worse. I'd stayed with her the entire time and she sort of semi imprinted onto me afterwards as her carer.

After the military shit I'd been through in the desert over the past few years, being kind to someone rather than too harsh felt...oddly good. Maybe the rescue in this case wasn't DD after all.

"You gonna day dream about your gourds all day? Maybe you get enough time with all your curves there, huh?" Anson didn't know when to give up.

I rolled my lips inward as Miss Daisy D gave me a fixed look that said *don't murder him in my paddock, please*.

"Never, ma'am," I muttered.

"D'you just call the horse, *ma'am?*" Ash Rhodes, the man who ran the Off-Duty Rescue Ranch, clapped a hand across my shoulder blades.

I stiffened. Daisy sent me a commiserating look.

"Is there a problem with how I address a beautiful lady?" I stroked Daisy's nose. She whickered in response, nuzzling me gently.

"She's taken to you," Ash mused. "I know a girl who did that once. You want to look after this one for me?"

I stroked Daisy's nose while something uncertain

coiled too tight in my gut, something that might shatter at a moment's notice.

Something akin to trust, unfounded.

"You know I can't be here most nights if she needs me," I said carefully. "And I care in the afternoons. Not that I'm not grateful. It's just that—" I paused, knowing his eyes were upon me. Knowing I couldn't screw up this chance at a slice of peace, of something *more* than the drifter life that had taken me from one ranch to the next, following the seasons for the last few years. This was the first place I'd had a glimpse of what home might feel like again in a long time and I'd do almost anything not to jeopardise that.

Plus, I had a sense of purpose here. A sense of something more than just place.

"You like the part of you that you've found here. And in town. I know that," Ash said, so easily. Much more so than I'd be able to say for myself. That rankled, but I held my silence and let the other, slightly older man finish. "I'm glad you're here with us, Elijah Campise. Both Off duty and Forest Grove wouldn't be the same without you."

I ground my teeth, unsure why his acceptance, when I couldn't do the same for myself, bothered me so much. "Appreciate it." I kept on stroking Daisy's nose long after Ash walked away, humming softly to her, unsure who was comforting who.

When I finished up with Daisy, had her settled for the afternoon, the yard stood empty, covered in long shadows, the glitter bus with its bare bear nowhere in sight.

And that meant it was time to get some real work done.

The night sky of Forest Grove hung over me as I sat out the back of *Gourd for You*, the patisserie I owned a fifty percent share of real estate in with Declan Evans. He baked, I carved. Gourds, mostly, by hand. None of this machine based stuff. I could control the designs if I did everything by hand, creating lace-work on the outside of the hard shell. Okay, so some-times I baked. Declan did the really hard stuff, and I made fun shapes that fit inside lamp-like gourds that grew on the property where I worked during the day.

Moonlighting as a carving patisserie chef didn't leave me a whole lot of sleeping hours, but it kept the nightmares away that had plagued me for a whole lot of years, and Ash allowed me the time off the ranch, so I made use of it all.

The gourd I held tonight was the traditional, elongated shape. Hollow in the middle, it looked a whole lot heavier than it actually was. They could be used to carry water, but I used to use them for art. This one would hold a family of capybara pastries when it was done that would be ready for the weekend trade. Declan had the designs, and the fillings for me. Chocolate was one of his specialities, while I loved working with the intricate patterns on both the gourds and the sugary pastry.

"I'm closing up for the night. Are you gonna be out here for a while longer, yet?" Declan raked his sugar encrusted fingers through his dark hair, leaving white stripes through the middle.

I grinned, the pressures of today having left me hours before. Carving and being out here always left me more relaxed than even being out on the ranch, where I'd thought I was happiest. Until I found this place, and Declan. His story wasn't so different from my own. A drifter with a slightly different history, but the same end result. We bought in on the same dream and suddenly we had a shop together. He ran it full time and I came in to hope out most nights.

I nodded, leaning my head back to stare up at the night sky that the small town's lights obscured. "You know you're always welcome up the ranch if you want a break."

"Now why would I do somethin' stupid like that?" Declan drawled, looking down at me. "Just because you found some friendlies, doesn't mean I have to share them with you."

I huffed a laugh. "Whatever, old man. Go home and get your beauty sleep"

He shoved his hands into his pockets. "Might need that. Did you see who moved into the flat above next door? Prettiest little thing. I thought I might ask her out for a drink tomorrow night. Unless you want to crash my party."

I made a face at him. "I promise I'll make myself scarce. And stay up at the ranch. You gonna close early, then?" On occasion we did a roaring night trade for a tiny, small town, catching people after work when they couldn't get away from their daily duties.

"Yeah, I thought I might."

"Don't get all broken hearted if she turns you down," I warned him. "I remember how your last romance went."

Declan sent me a wounded look. "Kimberly was a fine lass, thank you muchly."

"Except that she ran off with that banker from

the city about a month later." I looked down at my gourd, turning it around my hand. I'd finished one side, and had the next to go. Symmetry was a big thing with me.

"Yeah, that wasn't great" Declan scratched his chin as I looked back up at him.

"Go home, D. You're making my neck sore."

"Whiner," he mumbled, yawning. "See you in a few days for your bog cabybuddy thing."

"Capybara Gourd lighting," I corrected him, knowing he knew the name full well and was taking the piss. "Sleep well for your date."

"Eh, she hasn't said yes yet."

"Have you met her?" I called to his back.

He waved, a one fingered saluted in my direction as he walked away, locking the front door behind him.

I grinned, looked down at my gourd and concentrated on making the pattern match up to the shape in my hands, but damn if I couldn't get my mind off the girl with the curves who'd been at the Off-Duty ranch back earlier in the day, the girl with pretty curves all of her own who I knew shouldn't be about the ranch, or me, but craved anyway. The girl I'd fantasize about unhealthily for the next few hours.

My glitter bomb.

CHAPTER TWO

CADANCE

I stood outside the patisserie next to my rented upstairs room and reconsidered my life choices for all of a second. I mean, it came down to the pink glitter truck that really did stand out like a sore thumb parked out the front of our combined business and sleeping areas, and the chef in the patisserie who doubled as a cowboy during his noon moonlighting hours.

You know, the one who carved gourds and waltzed about the inside of his shop wearing jeans and an apron.

And that was all.

My mind really didn't take that much time to

decide on who to ask for help after I sucked in that delectable sight, all the pretty gourd carvings that littered his windows with their delectable, sugared treats inside.

Oh, and the knife buried hilt deep inside my flat tire. Which was why I stood outside the gourd-chef's shop at midnight, ready to beg for help.

Not because he looked good without a shirt, or because his other assets bulged as he finished carving up his current artwork. That took a significant amount of talent as well as a steady, gentle hand. Even I could see that.

Some of the larger displays nearest the window that I loitered near looked like pure lace around the edges. He'd placed lights behind and even inside some to illuminate the thinnest layers as well as the sugar encrusted pastry creations nestled inside. Tiny creatures of the woodlands featured there: squirrels, robins, a spotted deer. Even a wild turkey. And those weren't guesses. The depiction in pastry was clear, his stunning art work surrounding the mouth-watering dessert just as delectable.

And then there was the man himself.

Bulging kind of everywhere, covered in powdered sugar, the occasional fleck of paint from his alternative creation, his dark eyes focussed on the work in his hands.

And if I hadn't already had a bit of a hand fetish...welp, I sure as all get out did by now.

Long fingered, rough and calloused and all things both gentle and firm. *Swoon me sideways and pass me a gourd carving cowboy artist pastry chef, pretty please.*

Clearly, this was the perfect man to ask to change my tire, once I stopped perving on him.

I blinked, but the shop was empty.

Damnit, I missed my chance.

But there he was, dressed—well, dressed. As in, wearing a shirt. A long sleeved, black Henley, done up to the neck except for those top two buttons that were left open. Somehow, being dressed was all the more sexier on him.

What did you expect, Cadance? That he'd head back to his dude ranch wearing an apron and jeans?

Maybe my ovaries had hoped that was the case, but my logical brain—that appeared to have gone on hiatus the moment he appeared in the middle of the kitchen like an oversized, cowboy wraith.

Gone was the gourd-perv-worthy chef of moments before, when I'd vague out over carving hands and bulging biceps. Okay, so I starved for male specimens to ogle. Which, naturally, was why I was in this mess to begin with. You'd think that was enough to cure me of over active ovaries to start with, but apparently not.

My mouth opened as Mr tall, dark and Gourdy strode toward the door, keys in hand, where I'd been waiting on the other side all night. I did the only logical thing I could think of in that moment.

I ran.

And hid near the side of the building where mine adjoined his. It wasn't like I'd been practicing my speech for the past twenty minutes in my head or anything like that while I loitered out the front of his ship like a stalker instead of knocking, waxing and asking for help on the mostly deserted—okay, completely deserted— street front.

Nope. I acted like a complete stalker, unsure if I liked his display better, or him. The retail manager in me adored the display. The one hundred percent female in me appreciated the man. Could I just love both? Who knew. Instead, I cowered in the tiny space between buildings, thinking how stupid this whole scenario was.

I should go back up my stairs to my brand new rental, lock myself in, and deal with the vandalism in the morning. I was sure the locals would have a damn fine and logical reason why a knife was implanted into my tire. The distraction might cost me a day's trade but hey, maybe I could run my wax and nail service from the street front and use it to drum up business where I'd parked earlier in the afternoon instead of running appointments as a door to door service—

An oversized hand folded around my shoulder, yanked me from my hiding place, and a serrated knife crushed my windpipe to a mere thread of breathing space. Dark eyes I barely recognized from the gourd patisserie fixed on mine in an unyielding stare.

"You've got three seconds to tell me why you're out here," he rasped, digging the blade against my throat.

I swore flesh parted and life blood drizzled like frosting over my skin.

The hulk of a man bore his weight down on me. Actually, he kind of towered. My distant view from outside his window didn't do the enormity of this man, in all his glory, any form of justice. Any pithy words I wanted to speak in my defence of my midnight perving habits came out in a rush of breath and part of a squeak.

Holy hells, I hope he can change a tire after this.

And hot on the heels after that thought: that knife handle does not match the one jammed into my truck wheel.

At least my logical brain was still on its game while the rest of me was in freeze-prey mode.

My pathetic little mouse sound slipped between us like a whisper. A whisper that echoed along the otherwise silent street while my mountain man cowboy glared at me with some serious intent in his eyes.

Who the hell hurt this man, and what did I have to do to make it better?

His intense gaze sharpened, and with that focus the man I thought I recognized returned.

"What the hell were you doing out the front of my shop at this time of night, glitter bomb?" he seethed.

Ah, okay. So maybe he got grumpy after midnight. I wondered what would happen if I added water.

"I'm your neighbor. Upstairs," I added helpfully, darting my eyes sideways since I couldn't move, didn't dare breathe, and hoped that he wouldn't get a case of the jitters any time real soon. "I own the Bare Bear Travelling salon."

He bared his teeth in what might have been a

smile, but came off as only a little terrifying. "I noticed, glitter girl. I saw your van at the Off-Duty ranch earlier. Why the hell are you out here at this time of night?"

I put on my prettiest, best, most sparkly emergency smile. "Someone impaled my tire. I hoped you might help me change it before work tomorrow."

"What?"

I took a deep breath, and ran into the edge of his blade. "Help, please." I pressed my hand to his forearm, tracing corded tendons strung tight over hard musculature beneath.

His gaze flicked downward, and the blade retracted. "Fuck. I didn't—" He raked the scarred, whitened knuckles of the hand still gripping the serrated blade through his hair, leaving the ends in a haphazard mess. Sugar dusted his shoulders.

"I'm sorry, Ca—" His teeth snapped together like a bear trap had been set off.

I would have winced, if I hadn't been invested in catching that little slip. "You know my name?"

He ignored me, sheathing the knife at his back and reached out. His hands brushed my skin in the lightest touch, then he drew back. "May I?"

I barked out a laugh, disturbing the night on the silent street a second time. "It's a bit late now, isn't it?" and far too late for me, the shivers set in, a delayed reaction of what had just happened.

"I'm sorry." One arm braced against the bricked shop wall behind my head as he dipped his head and studied the damage he'd created.

I held back tears—just—as he swiped a fingertip across my throat. I swore that imprint would come up bloodied, but when he showed me proof, all I saw was skin the same as the rest of his hand: scarred from a lifetime doing who knew what, if a knife large enough to take on the proverbial bear was his first thought, coated with residual sugar from tonight's activities. The two actions were so at odds with each other, a dichotomy in this man, that for a moment, all I could do was stare.

"You're okay," he coaxed, shifting his bulk as he eased closer. "Cadance," —all facades were dropped there about knowing who I was— "I'm sorry I scared you. I thought— Well, it doesn't matter what I thought. I shouldn't have reacted like that, not on a street. Not here, and not with someone... Not with you," he finished, keeping his voice soft, regular. His thumb brushed back and forth across my throat in a smooth motion I didn't want to break, but his words slammed into my mind like a fresh trauma slap.

I peered up at him through slitted eyes.

"What's so wrong about someone *like me*?" I asked, my own voice far from calm as the edges of panic set in. "I just needed a tire changed, that's all."

"And you couldn't come in and ask like a normal person?" The corner of his mouth flickered up.

"No, Elijah. I couldn't," I sassed him.

It wasn't until the hand still stroking back and forth across my throat where his blade had been breaths before that I realized how much I'd screwed up.

Oh, fuckity.

I rallied my best fake ass smile again.

"Apparently, I know your name, too."

CHAPTER THREE

ELIJAH

I stared at the knife embedded in the back tire of Cadance's glitter van parked behind my black RAM 3500. When I'd discovered that the naked bear had taken up residence outside the shop I moonlighted as both carver and baker, I took the opportunity to get to know my new neighbor.

Cadance Webster appeared in Forest Grove a little less than a week ago with exactly zero history to her created name. Ask me how I recognized that little non-existent trail. I had one that matched for the first few years of my return to the country after my deployments overseas with the military. Once I came home, I couldn't keep my feet still. Sold up everything I had, packed what I actually needed into the back of my truck, and hit the road.

For three years, I didn't stop running. Not until I hit Montana a while back, and worked a few seasons up north at a place called Red Hart Ranch. The quiet spread of the land and towering mountain backdrop there reminded me of how small I was, and returned something to me that I'd lost a long time back in another country:

Perspective.

And so when my seasons there were up, I said goodbye to the ranch owners, Eve and Travis, a pair of twins who ran their land on loyalty and damn good food. When I hit the road again, it was with a fresh set of eyes, and the sort of pace I could maintain for a whole lot longer.

And when I met Declan in town, then started working at the Off Duty ranch, I knew my feet would be able to stay still for a while longer. That it might be time to risk putting down roots again.

All that to say, when I stared at the knife embedded in Cadance's tire, the glitter truck she'd designed around her pell-mell style life that never seemed to stop and the risks she took without any consideration of consequences, I wondered just how long the woman who waited at my back had been running, and from who.

Hell, it was after midnight, and she never twigged that it seemed strange to ask me for help, standing outside my shop. Or that I hadn't said no to her. Her sense of normality was as skewed as mine had been, once. It was all too easy to fall back into that stance with her, staring at the problem, finding the solution.

Finding a reason not to send her away.

Because hadn't that been the reason I'd found out so much about her in the first place, that she'd stuck in my mind ever since I saw her at the ranch? Daisy Duke was a mighty fine horse, but even her chestnut hide couldn't take my mind off the curves the woman who waited behind me had. Curves that left me breathless just standing near her.

And I'd fucking well hurt her, because instinct, honed and all too well practiced, had taken over before my mind caught up with the present. I'd reacted to the threat outside my shop forgetting that there was no *threat* here. But my body responded the way it'd been trained; not to think, only to survive.

And so I drew the blade I still couldn't bear not to wear, and nearly sliced her flawless skin open.

My thumb brushed across the top of the handle

of the blade in her tire. I pulled my hand back fast, and shook my head to dispel the memory of touching her after. That she'd *let me*, when she should have been screaming or passed out in terror.

"This isn't just vandalism, is it?" she asked in the kind of quiet voice that told me her natural buoyancy had been muted before.

Probably by the person she suspected had done the deed, and now she wondered if they'd found her.

Who are you running from, glitter bomb?

But she wouldn't tell me if I asked her outright. I knew that, because for years I'd held my own trauma too close, worn it as a mark of guilt, and pride, but hadn't been ready to discard either. And every time someone got close, closer than a one night stand or offered friendship, I did what anyone high on the fast lane of life did.

I ran.

As far and as wide as this country allowed.

I'd worked ranches and towns from one end to the other, rarely crossing my own path in the same calendar year and never crossing over with the same crowd once. That's how I knew that if I pushed Cadance Webster on who she was hiding from right now, in the morning, she'd be gone and I'd be responsible for a naked bear covering its privates on a very public street front.

Instead, I nodded, giving her what she wanted, but probably didn't want to believe.

"Yeah, it's not random vandalism. And from what I know of this town, random acts don't happen like this. Not unless there's a grudge match worthy of it." I shut my damn mouth hard enough to leave my jaw aching, but if there was more information in the works on this side of midnight, then she'd have to give a little to get a little.

"That happens."

I felt her shrug, more than saw it. My thighs screamed from crouching low in the street for too long as I pushed up to standing. "You got a spare? Tools?" I had my own, but looking at the make and model of her van, it'd likely require manufacturer's tools that matched her vehicle to fit.

"Yes. They're here." She opened the back of her van, and I was assaulted by a dangling disco ball that flung scattered white light into my eyes. "Oh. Sorry. It's a bit..."

"Overwhelming is the word you're looking for," I said dryly as she scrambled to peel back the matching pink glitter linoleum that lined the base of the van. The sides were covered in fold away compartments, each color coded to match that held an assortment of beauty treatments and products from their neat labels. The woman was a single person army.

"I know, I match," she sighed as she stepped aside and waved a hand tiredly at her skinny, partially delaminating spare tire. "Taa-daa."

I blinked at the unusable spare, my throat tightening. "Actually, I'd call you formidable. And that's... not gonna work, glitter bomb. You got time for a coffee? Cause we're gonna need to make a plan for tomorrow. And I don't think you can stay here tonight. Not if you think this wasn't a random act of violence."

She didn't answer me.

I glanced up, certain, for a moment, that she'd done as I predicted already and I'd be staring at a blank spot on the pavement beside her van.

But she wasn't. I held her wide, cinnamon eyes that met mine over the knuckles stuffed in her mouth. There'd be bite divots in those knuckles, and it set my shoulders in a tight line that she felt she couldn't let out the scream she so obviously stifled.

I peeled her flooring back, keeping my face averted, giving her time to breath, if she could. If she couldn't... Well, we'd deal with that in a second.

Finally, I locked up the back of her van after checking she had a key. The faintest nod was my only response. Cadance had checked out, and it wasn't because of me or that damn knife, but it was a close thing. Worse, I didn't have a puncture kit, which meant the offending article would have to stay right where it was for the time being. At least until I organized a tow for her in the morning and someone to fix it. If she'd let me.

I faced her, my mouth set in a line that matched my shoulders. Because I knew sure as shit she wouldn't like this next part one bit.

"Alright, glitter bomb. Time to show me which door is yours, and talk me through what's happening in your life that leads to your van being ruined in a town that you weren't in last week."

With respect, I knew most of that, including which door was hers, but she didn't need to know that right now. And I still expected her to run at any moment.

As before, Cadance surprised me, holding out her hand. "Come on," she said softly. "I'll show you."

I raised both eyebrows. Cadance Webster was made of the sort of dreams that made a man want to change his own to match hers. Maybe that was what had her running from place to place, changing who she'd been and reinventing herself behind glowing personas that were fake as fuck.

Because the glitter bomb in front of me was both the woman underneath, and not. I promised myself that by the end of the night, I'd know who she was, and who she'd been.

And how the hell she learned my name.

Because all of a sudden, that little piece of info seemed mighty important.

CHAPTER FOUR

CADANCE

Elijah barely fit in my cramped rental apartment, the last one in the packed town that seemed all but closed to new arrivals. Oh, sure, the people were welcoming—to an extent. Super friendly, right up until I asked for the best place to set up shop and stay. Then those smiles became fixed, and frayed at the edges.

I recognized those fragile expressions. I'd worn them more often than not in a previous life. Not the one that I existed in now. At least, not until tonight.

I'd thought I could hide for a while longer. Pretend that the life I had lived wouldn't catch me quite so fast. But apparently six months, three weeks and four days was the limit of my reprieve, if I counted today.

And somehow, I didn't think I should.

"How long have you been running?" Elijah didn't beat around the bush. Large, scarred hands that bore tiny cracks across his knuckles held his coffee mug still. He hadn't taken cream or sugar, and I wanted desperately to rub moisturizer into the backs of his hands.

But I folded my fingers around my own mug and tried to channel some of his unfathomable stillness instead. "I don't know your last name," I blurted, like that was the critical piece of information between us that was missing.

The corner of his mouth quirked. "Your research didn't tell you that much?" his head tipped to one side as he watched me, but I kept my mouth shut. Finally, he sighed. "It's Campise." He made that last sound like another '*i*'.

"I checked on all my neighbors," I mumbled into my mug, turning it in circles. There was no point trying to sit still like him. It just wasn't in me to do. Thankfully, Elijah didn't put his hands over mine and try to make me sit still like...someone else used to.

He huffed out a breath. "That must have made you popular. This town likes its secrets."

I managed a watery smile, the pressure of the night and the invasion of reality on my little pretend bubble finally cracking through my fake smile facade that I'd held up for six solid months and change. "Just as much as they liked the idea of me moving in here, I guess."

Rough fingers brushed my curls back from my face. The frizz that must have been a messy mass, similar to the unruly halo I woke up with most days, bounced right back where it was, earning me another huff of a laugh.

"I can imagine," he murmured, coiling one frizzed out curl around his finger, then unwinding it again. His eyes unfocused with the motion, like it mesmerized him. Heat emanated from his hand, and I swallowed back the need to lean into his touch, but held back, stealing the moment to study his face.

Before, when we'd been outside his shop, fear and adrenaline prevented me from soaking in anything beyond survivalism. Now, in the relative safety of my new, albeit smaller space of a home, I had the luxury of tracing the lines around his mouth with my eyes, how the green in his eyes warred with shards of yellow in a kaleidoscope of autumnal colors. Reds and dark browns shimmered in his hair, and a tan line where his hat sat low on his brow during the day kept his skin glowing.

But shadows flickered across his expression as he returned my study, and I knew I wasn't the only one who crowded my tiny kitchen table that had sustained damage. And suddenly, that tan line, the cracked knuckles and the scars on the backs of his hands, fine but there all the same made sense in a different sort of light.

"You were military. Weren't you?"

His winding fingers stilled, but he didn't let my hair go. "Does that mantle ever really fall away, even if you haven't worn the uniform for a while?" he murmured.

The question seemed aimed inwards, rather than at me, so I didn't try to answer it for him. I wondered if he had ever tried to answer it for himself.

"How long have you been here?" I asked instead, since he seemed to be in question mode, and hoped he'd answer.

"A few years here, more out there." He tugged on my hair, drawing me closer. "I tried to stop, even managed for a while. But nothing seemed to really stick. Then I came here. Met Declan. The baker next door," he said when I frowned, exposing the truth of my lie.

Oops.

"Okay, so maybe I only asked about one neighbor?" I offered.

Breath brushed my lips when I didn't pull away from him. "How long did you watch me tonight, glitter bomb?"

I blinked. "I– I have no idea."

"Even with someone around who wanted to damage your things? Hurt you?" His hand dropped to cradle my jaw. The action was undeniably intimate, removing all playfulness from the interaction. I struggled to breathe this close to him. "You stood with your back to the street for how long, Cadance?"

The use of my name jolted me back to reality.

I jerked away from his hold, but he didn't let me, closing his fingers across my nape in a firm but unbreakable grip. "Let go," I whispered, but my protest wavered with each word.

"Tell me," he countered, his eyes flashing a warning at me.

I shook my head, restless in his hold even though I fought myself more than him. "A prison is still a prison, even if you've bribed me with secrets and pretty stories," I managed, knowing this wouldn't stop because he'd only let me go if I said so.

We both knew I wouldn't.

"How long?" he murmured, angling his mouth over mine.

"I don't know."

"Better," he breathed at my confession.

At least one of us can breathe. That was my last coherent thought before his mouth descended over mine. Then I couldn't think at all.

Only feel.

Rough hands tangled through my curls with infinite care as he leaned into me. His kisses weren't hesitant or too rough, but firm, telling me what he knew I needed. What my body ached for, what I craved.

Who I craved.

Someone to hold me in arms that didn't band too tight, but held me firmly as he lifted me onto his hips, let me straddle him as his hands I'd observed earlier grazed over the curves of my ass. The way his mouth moved against mine, firm but coaxing, gentle but demanding, matched my own need.

I opened for him as he cupped my hips, helping me find the rhythm that stole my breath before his tongue invaded my mouth and my world shrank to a slow awareness of only sensation and singular breath when he allowed it.

My choked moan, a muted sound as I found the hard ridge of him between my legs, left me in a frenzy of need. He didn't stop me as I rubbed harder against him, but he didn't rush our kisses, either, slowing the place until I sighed against him, letting my weight rest against his chest.

When I came, a hot gush of liquid that coated my panties and thighs inside my jeans that I wished was on his hand instead, he held me close to his chest. Elijah's kisses turned languid as I panted against his mouth, letting me rock out the last waves of my pleasure against his body.

His lips grazed my cheek as he pulled back once my breaths evened out. I gazed up at him through dozy eyes, seeing only a man who stared down at me with eyes full of need and possession. A second dose of lust spiked through me as he traced my tingling, swollen lips.

"Fuck, that was beautiful, glitter bomb." He tugged me closer. "You gonna go to sleep on my lap?"

I mewled against him, straining for more of those addictive kisses, knowing he wanted more, just like I did. "I have a bed," I rasped helpfully, unable to find my voice. I held a yawn behind my hand.

He laughed softly. "And if we crawl into your bed, I'll fuck you until the sun rises, Cadance."

"That doesn't sound like so bad an option."

"Except that dawn isn't that far away. Rest, glitter girl. I'll wake you before I gotta leave, okay?"

When I know you're safe.

He didn't need to say it. We both heard his words. I nodded tiredly, nestling my cheek into his shoulder.

I'm not the only one who needs a little TLC.

A few hours ago, or maybe half a dozen of them, this man held a knife to my throat. He held his own history of scars and damage that would take plenty of time to sift through, if he was even willing to share beyond the surface of what we'd touched tonight in the smallest hours when everyone else in Forest Grove were in their beds.

But Elijah Campise gave me his name. He trusted me that far, that easy. Maybe I should return the favor. So I did what he wanted, and let the world fade away in the arms of the cowboy that I still wasn't sure if I should trust or not. With hands the ones that cradled me like it was the most precious art work he'd ever carved, who was I to argue?

CHAPTER FIVE

ELIJAH

The glitter mystery machine cost a small fortune to repair, not that I'd tell Cadance that. I had plenty in my savings to cover the cost of her European build van that required tires that would have to be shipped in overnight to the small town.

From what I'd seen of her apartment last night, the chipped, second hand furniture that must have been sourced from every garage sale this last week in Forest Grove, I doubted Cadance had more than a few bucks left to her name right now.

And I wondered if her violent little stalker knew

just how close she was to running dry on everything
—funds, energy, even pluck.

I saw that in her last night when I kissed her, felt
in the way she fell into my arms. The moment I
offered her a little TLC, she submitted to everything
I needed from her, opening to my kisses, gave me
everything I demanded from her.

It'd been all too easy to rile her up into a hot mess
on my lap. She'd cum for me in mere minutes, rolling
her hips over mine until I thought I wouldn't be able
to hold my own need back. It'd been damn close with
her, the way she'd ridden me with pure abandon.

I hadn't been so reckless since I returned from
military service. There'd been a few women over the
years, sure, but none, not one, was like her.

I could still feel the warmth of her curves etched
into my palms, how she'd leaned into my touch the
moment I encouraged her. The worst part? I knew
she was my new addiction. Even though I shouldn't
take advantage of the woman who latched herself to
the first person who showed an interest in her, who
touched her with care, I couldn't help it.

Tonight, I knew I'd go back to her, rather than
stay at the ranch after I was done there like I should.
Was it taking advantage if we both needed it? Hell, I
didn't know any more. The mechanic before me was

still talking about her glitter van, and I hadn't heard a word he'd said, lost in my daydream of the pretty girl riding my cock with too many layers of denim crushed between us mere hours before.

And tonight I'd damn well make sure there wouldn't be anything but bare skin between her pretty pussy and my fingers and tongue.

The mechanic looked up at me expectantly, and gave me an encouraging nod.

I knew then that his price was more than I wanted to hear, but I'd pay it anyway because she needed to have that van running to make her on-the-road beauty business work. I understood that part all too well, the need for independence.

"Tell me again what's wrong with it?" I muttered, promising myself I'd pay attention this time and concentrate on the pink glitter monstrosity in front of me instead.

The mechanic rattled off a list of internal faults apart from the single damaged tire. I winced as he kept going happily and knew I was in for a long negotiation before I could head back to the ranch for the afternoon.

"I always did wonder if the gourd business would cross over with your duties here." Ash watched me with his arms folded across his chest like he knew exactly what I wasn't telling him.

Daisy Duke whickered at my shoulder. I stroked her nose gently. "It's one night." My voice strained. I wasn't sure if it was from the outright lie, or the omission I refused to say.

Ash nodded. "Uh huh. And one night will become two. Two nights will become a week. What's her name, again?"

I smirked. "Did you think I'd give it up that easily?"

He shrugged. "I could try. So I'm worried about the wrong thing, then?"

My shoulders cracked as I rolled them. Daisy wandered away in search of fresh grass or another cowboy to fetch her treats. "Maybe. But point taken anyway."

Ash watched me a while longer. If he was waiting for me to get fidgety, he was shit out of luck. Finally, he blew out a breath. "You've got a cabin here for as long as you want it. You know that, soldier."

I nodded. "I know that." He'd never drawn rank into a conversation before, and service talk was usually off the table, unless the conversation called for it. Apparently this one did, which meant that my feet were about to get itchy real damn fast. "Looks like I'm due back in town about now, then."

Ash didn't contradict me or try to stop me as I walked away, but by the time I climbed into the cab of my truck, my feet were a little less itchy, and I wondered if I wasn't doing the wrong thing heading back into to town for a fling that wouldn't last more than a few weeks at most when my heart was set on a piece ranch land that Ash offered with no strings attached.

Usually I carved in the evenings as a way to keep the tremors out of my hands that seemed to come on with the bouts of exhaustion I worked into my bones at the ranch. There were more technical and mechanized ways to do it, but holding the chisel and lathe in my hands, working through the designs I drew on myself, calmed something in my mind, a lot like hyper focus, I guessed. Something that took all the white noise and chatter and pushed it back for a few more hours. Then, like I did with Cadance last night, I could finally sit still.

Those scant hours late at night were hard earned, but worth every minute to get there.

Tonight, however, I baked. Or, more to the point, I prepared. Because when Cadance walked through the doors I left unlocked just for her, I wanted her to find my shop—absent of Declan, who took the night off to give me space I requested—covered in a huge mess. Part of me wanted to see what she'd say. The other part of me had different plans.

While I waited for my newest addiction, I wrapped up a particular sugared treat with a sweet strawberry centre from last year's local crop that Declan and I had stewed large batches into a compote and frozen them, and now it was time for their use.

I'd just taken the first batch out of the oven when the shop door swung inward. Not a tentative opening, nor did I expect her to be gentle this time around. Cadance had topped up her sparkly little love tanks last night. Now she seemed energized and I couldn't wait to see what the real woman underneath was like when she shed the cumulative months or years of fear, what running on pure adrenaline had done to her when she got to be herself again and could simply *feel*.

I knew I couldn't achieve all that in just one

night but damned if I wouldn't give it my best. And the pretty little baked critter on the bake tray before me was my offering on a sugared altar to her.

"What's it meant to be?" Cadance peered around my arm as I dusted the fat, four legged, strawberry filled critter with sugar.

I grimaced. "It's *supposed* to be the first in a batch of a family of capybaras. But this one didn't turn out quite the way it should." I poked at the oversized snout, and a little strawberry oozed out.

Cadance swiped the drop onto her fingertip and poked it into her mouth before I could warn her about burning her tongue. Her eyes flew wide.

I winced, grabbing for a water bottle. "Here—"

"Oh, that's good, Elijah," she murmured appreciatively.

I turned to look at her, really look at her. A long cotton dress hung over her curves, obscuring the curves I knew hid beneath. She'd topped everything with a plain, faded denim jacket, slightly frayed at the edges, like she'd had it for a long time. I reached out and rubbed the hem between my fingers while she sucked strawberry jam from hers. The material was soft, confirming my theory.

"I wasn't sure you'd come to find me tonight, glitter bomb," I murmured, using the hem of her jacket to reel her in. I lifted the deformed pastry with my other hand, lifting it to a different bench, knowing I'd need the one behind me soon.

The finger in her mouth popped free. "Do you want me to go?" Her eyes widened, her gaze darting about the kitchen as she took in my work. "—I've interrupted you. I'm sorry. I'll go—"

"No." I caught her chin and directed her attention back to me. "Right now, I want you to take off that jacket you love so much and put it over there, on top of my recipe books. It's a safe place and it won't get ruined later. Then I want you to come back here to me, alright?"

She licked her lips. "Then what?"

I held her cinnamon gaze. "Then you're going to strip for me, get your stunning fucking ass up on that bench, and spread your legs so I can finally find out how sweet you are when you come on my tongue."

CHAPTER SIX

ELIJAH

Wide eyes stared back at me. For a moment, I wondered if I'd pushed my luck a touch too far. Then Cadance peeled off her jacket, her gaze never wavering from mine as she folded the faded denim into a neat square.

Cadance turned away to place her jacket where I showed her on top of my books, then turned back to me, running her fingers along the thin straps of her dress.

"Hold that thought." I swallowed hard and leaned back to dim the lights just enough to see slightly more than her silhouette.

If Cadance was going to strip for me, I wanted to see her, but I didn't want to scare any local townspeople out taking a late walk. She was already struggling for acceptance and while I could deal with a certain level of reputation, the local rumor mill in full production at Forest Grove would hurt her a hell of a lot more than it would me.

"Should we be somewhere less public?" She glanced at the front window that I'd overcrowded with display gourds earlier in the evening for exactly this reason.

"No, glitter bomb," I said softly. "I want to do this right here, tonight. Let me see you, because I want you spread open for me on that benchtop like a treat made just for me."

She shivered, one arm wrapping around herself. I held my breath, barely grazing my fingertips along her arm. Cadance lifted her chin and pushed one shoulder strap down with a flick coated in her personal brand of defiance. Against herself or me, I wasn't sure.

The other strap went next, and then the whole dress just slithered over her body like a sheath. And suddenly I was staring at an expanse of creamy, curved skin without a speck of lace or undergarments marring my sight. Rounded arms led to full breasts tipped with dusky, peaked nipples begging to be toyed with. I ached to know if she moaned or cried out if I sucked on them while I pushed my fingers into her bald pussy. Her tummy was rounded too, just perfectly so, to match her full hips and the ass I'd played with on my lap when she got herself off for me the night before. And there, against that perfect skin, was a wide patch of crisscrossed lines, thin where someone had hacked into her body, breaking that flawless skin. Suddenly I had my answer on her career choices, why she froze up that first night with me, and the act of defiance undressing just now.

My throat dried and I realized just how unprepared I was for this moment.

"Who did this to you, glitter bomb," I asked softly, raking my gaze over her body, seeking other damage. But anything else she hid was on the inside.

She shook back her glorious golden mane and met my gaze head on. "What you see is what you get, cowboy. I'm just one of thousands of women who picked the wrong man to marry. 'The safe one'." Her lips twisted into a smile I hated.

"He did this to you." My voice flattened. I tried to keep the anger away that bloomed low in me, but I couldn't keep it down. "Fuck, glitter bomb, I'll—"

"He doesn't matter. Nothing else does. Just us. Here. And your funky capybara pastry that tastes like strawberries and springtime." That blast of defiance was back in her eyes, daring me to defy her.

I didn't want to defy her. I wanted to fall to my knees and worship her like the mountain goddess she was destined to become. I opened my mouth, but nothing, not a single damn sound, came out.

"Am I too much?" She peeked at me from beneath thick, curled lashes, her blonde hair bobbing around her face. The faintest hint of a coy smile flickered at the corners of her lips like she knew the exact effect she had on me, standing there as bare as anything, scars and all, and proud of her survival. Hell, I was damn proud of her, too.

"You're never too much for me," I promised, unclenching my hands from my sides. I ached to touch her, but my brain jammed at the sight of her perfection right in front of me.

She seemed to get the message, and the hint of a smile became a full blown flirtation that knocked me back a step as she sashayed into me, hips swaying, hair tossed back, the whole deal.

Full breasts pressed to my chests as she rose up onto her toes. My hands were finally my own, grazing over those luscious as all fuck hips I'd dreamed about for the past few nights.

"Hells, glitter bomb. Can I touch, or am I on looking only duties?" I asked reverently.

"Touch me, please," she breathed, rising up as high as she could.

I caught her waist, sinking my fingers into her luscious curves and let out a groan. "You gonna let me live out the fantasy I planned now, glitter girl?" I pulled her close, letting her feel how tight the inside space of my jeans had become the moment she dropped that dress. "I'm gonna lift you up and turn around, okay? It might get a little cold."

She had a question in her eyes I answered with a quick kiss, squeezing her waist and lifted her off her feet. Breath whooshed from her, bringing a little squeak with it. Cadance laced her arms and legs around my neck and hips, clinging to me. I nearly gave up on the plan then and there, found a comfortable, spare piece of wall and fucked us into tomorrow.

But I had the plan, the fantasy laid out, and I wasn't about to break that when she was right here, pressed to me.

Cadance yelped when I placed her butt on the sugar dusted metal bench I'd clean up later, the unforgiving surface chill beneath her heated skin. She panted softly, her breasts rising and falling, nipples grazing my shirt as she stared up at me where I stood between her soft, curved thighs.

"What now?" she whispered, sinking back into herself.

"Uh uh, glitter bomb. You come right on back to me. I want to hear you tonight. Every damn moan," I murmured., pushing her thighs open wider.

She let me, her eyes curious as I knelt, palming her inner thighs to hold her wide for me, and licked her glistening folds. A gasp left her, and her palms slapped the bench top.

I hummed my approval. "Christ, you're sweet. That's it, Cadance, let me hear everything you feel. Show me what my girl likes."

She shivered above me as I traced the shape of her with my tongue, exploring gently. Her thighs quivered beneath my hands, tensing and pressing inwards when I found her sensitive spots or delved my tongue inside her hole, slowly fucking her and tasting her sweetness.

Her slick dripped lower. I lapped it up, unwilling to waste anything she gave me before I rose up to tap the tip of my tongue on her clit.

Cadance's head fell back, and she sighed, rolling

her hips up to meet my mouth. "Yes, please," she murmured.

Not begging, exactly, more dreamlike. I could work with that.

Scooping a fingertip's worth of dusted sugar from the bench, I brushed it across her clit and folds, then dipped my mouth to suckle it off. "Fuck, that's sweet, Cadance," I groaned, imagining her covered in the sticky strawberry mixture, and sucking it off her until she writhed for me, coming until she was clean again. I lapped at her clit as she shivered. Her thighs tensed against my palms and a keening cry broke from her lips. I sucked her clit into my mouth, pulsing my tongue over the tight bud, and she broke softly for me.

Her body arched, hands tangling in my hair as she rode her orgasm out on my face. Hell, if I could drown in her sweetness, I'd still be addicted to her taste. Cleaning her gently, I let her come down, freeing one hand to unbutton my shirt and shuck it onto the floor behind me. I worked a few buttons free on my jeans as I rose, tracing the shape of her throbbing flesh with my other hand.

She let me play, laying back across my benchtop. Her silky blonde hair hung off the edge in a golden cascade. I leaned over her body to dust her nipples with sugar then sucked it off, repeating the process until she gushed against my gentle fingers playing in her pussy.

"Fuck, you feel heavenly, glitter bomb," I murmured. "Gonna let me sink into you now? Can I fill you up bare?" I wanted to so damn bad, but I'd stop everything the moment she said so.

"I'm safe," she whispered. "I've got an implant and I haven't been able to be with...' her hand drifted across her tummy as her words failed.

I dusted sugar across the backs of her fingers, over her tummy and scars, then licked and sucked that off her skin too. "Every inch of you is so beautiful, Cadance," I rasped. "Every," —I notched my cock at her entrance— "Single," —I slid in an inch and waited as she gasped and writhed prettily for me— "Inch." I pushed home, all the way, eased by her slick heat.

Her pussy enveloped my length. I fought back the tingle that started low in my spine, working my cock in shallow thrusts until I managed control of my own body. Her soft cries told me I needed to be deeper inside her. I jacked my hips, snapping my thrust at the end, and revelled in her scream. Hell, that sound would live rent free in my head for months to come. I knew that, and I did the whole thing again, over and over, until she was gasping and twisting beneath me. Her pussy gripped my cock like a vice, milking me before her next orgasm had started.

I gritted my teeth, leaning down to suck her nipples. "You're so sweet, Cadance. I want to wake you up sucking on your nipples and see if you can come on my cock while I slide inside you every morning before you're fully awake. See how much you'll gush all over your thighs for me to lick up later, huh?"

She moaned, arching on my bench as her heat tightened inside. I couldn't breathe as she came, her pussy clamped down so tight I thought I'd found sweet heaven. Her scream in my ear as I gathered her in my arms, calling my name, was the last thing I remembered before I drove deep inside her and spend myself with her legs wrapped around my hips, and her nails digging into the back of my neck.

I lay there with her, both of us covered in sugar as her body offered the sort of warmth and softness I never wanted to leave.

"Fuck, glitter bomb. Next time, I'm taking you back to the ranch and you're staying in my cabin overnight. Alright?" I murmured into her skin, still intent on sucking and licking every inch of her.

"You have a cabin? That sounds nice," she breathed wistfully. I shifted my hips and she gasped, still super sensitive after coming so hard for me. "Damn, woman. I thought you were my new addiction. But licking you is my obsession." I slid out of her, slithered down her belly and licked my way to her pussy, lapping at her skin.

"No, what–" she stared, then moaned as my tongue lapped gently at her folds, cleaning her sweetly.

I worked my way back to her clit, circling the bud that tightened beneath my attention. Her hands tangled in my hair, showing me exactly what she needed this time. I smiled against her tender flesh, working her until she burst for me. Her screams rasped, voice strained and I knew she was done, if for now.

Standing on straining legs of my own, I scooped her into my arms, and headed into the downstairs shower, flicking it on. "You like a hot shower?"

"Mhmm," she murmured drowsily.

I laughed, giddy with the pure pleasure of having given her what I hoped she wanted most. Cadance crashed against me as I washed her gently, cleaning the stickiness off her body, making sure she stayed warm as I washed her hair. She curled against my chest as I washed myself, then wrapped her in a thick towel of my own.

"You gonna come upstairs with me?" I asked softly. "Sometimes I sleep here. Thought it might be easiest since your van will probably be ready tomorrow. I'll work at the ranch and then come back to get you, okay?"

She nodded, her eyes half closed as she followed me up the stairs, her hand clasped in mine. I'd have to repeat that to her tomorrow, but that was okay. I'd take whatever time she needed. Cadance Webster was my glitter bomb and making her smile was my mission.

Maybe tonight we could catch a little shut eye, too.

CHAPTER SEVEN

CADANCE

My breath matched the bear who slept beneath me. Not a bare bear, because this one slept in shorts, though I apparently opted to drift off naked. I peeked open an eye and found myself in a bedroom I didn't know, the haze before dawn still hanging over the room, even though the curtains weren't drawn.

"It's my room, glitter bomb." Elijah stroked my hair down my back. The curls had no doubt fallen out long ago. Actually they felt a bit damp. I pressed a hand to my head and came up with the sensation of a frizzy mess. "What did we do–"

Elijah's chest rumbled beneath me. "I washed your hair last night, afterward."

"You did?" I didn't remember that. Mind, I didn't remember much after several orgasms of the mind blowing variety. I certainly didn't remember ending up in his bed in his house...I only remembered the kitchen and his mouth on me, sucking sugar from my body and ....

Oh God, can that man do things with his tongue.

My cheeks blazed as I hid my head against his chest. A small moan left my lips as heat rushed across my chest and pooled between my thighs.

Elijah laughed again, rolling us. His knees spread my legs wide, and he slid inside me, eased by that fresh wave of heat that slicked the deeper places between my thighs. I moaned, clawing his chest from pure pleasure. Everything was celebrated with him. Taste, sensation, heat...it was like an oven turned up to ten in every sense.

My moan turned into a whine as he withdrew, leaving only the tip of his cock inside me. I blinked up at him, bereft. A moment before I couldn't remember half of last night. Now, I needed him to fill me, be back inside me more than anything in this world.

"Beg," he grated, staring down at me with the

same possession in his eyes as he had that first night he'd kissed me. "I want to hear you, Cadance."

I'd played games like this before, with another man, but then they'd been perfunctory. Because back then, I'd felt a sense of duty. With Elijah, a thrill raced through me at the way he looked down at me like it was the most fascinating and precious creature he'd ever seen.

I also had the impression that if I didn't do as he asked, he'd pull away and leave me with a cheeky slap on the rump, just for giggles. That was the flip side of this man. His crazy matched mine, and I loved that about him.

My breath caught in my throat. *What the hell?* A few days ago I was perving on him. Now I was falling for the pastry chef who made cute animal shapes? Mind, with a tongue like that...

But it was more than his tongue the way he looked at me, held me... Elijah Campise was the sort of man I knew I'd fall for hard and fast. Hell, if I admitted it to myself, I was already halfway there. He put me before his own needs more than once already and it had been a long, long time since anyone else had done that.

The last time I trusted someone, he drove everyone else in my life away, leaving me on an island with just him. I was okay with that.... until I realized that island was a prison and he was my warden in the sort of hell I had never signed up for.

Elijah.... Was nothing like that. Not from the parts of himself he'd shown me, and not from what I'd heard about him around town. The man who came in and gave people pure happiness with his art and cooking. Who helped out with rescue horses.

Who helped me.

"Cadance, I'd better hear you begging me damn fast, beautiful," he warned me, flexing his hips.

I gasped, arching towards him, but he pulled back and the sensation of him filling me disappeared. I mewled, knowing already that he loved the sound. "I need you, please," I started.

"Better," he approved. "More, glitter bomb. Make it filthy."

I recalled the way he'd made me come from his words alone the night before, and added a little flex from my pussy as a teaser. He growled, letting me know I'd pushed too far but hey, that's what I did and it usually got me in shit. I was okay with that with him, because somewhere over the last few days, we'd established trust and I knew he wouldn't hurt me.

"I want you so deep that the feel of you is all I

need," I whispered, letting my eyes close, imagining him that deep inside me. "So deep that when I wrap my legs around you and rock down, you're deeper than anyone has ever been—"

He growled and slammed hilt deep inside me on a roar. A shriek tore from my lips as I took him, hot and slicked and unprepared for the invasion.

"Fuck. Did I hurt you?" He cradled my face between his palms. "Tell me I didn't hurt you." Worried eyes met mine.

I shook my head. "Perfect, Eli," I murmured. "Don't stop?"

Another rumble from his chest broke free as he moved again, but this time when he withdrew it wasn't all the way. Our bodies crashed back together, over and over, until sweat pooled between us, creating little rivulets.

I clung to his neck, letting him ride out his need into me. Every muscle tensed, strong and powerful as he moved, knowing exactly what he wanted, and took it. My legs wrapped around his hips, and he let me hold onto him. One hand gripped my hip, his thumb sliding into the soft, sensitive join there. I moaned as he rested his weight on me, driving deeper. Elijah lifted my legs over one shoulder, flexing my back.

"Hold on," he muttered through gritted teeth. "This is going to be fast, glitter bomb."

I dug my nails into his hardened biceps for purchase. He hadn't lied, railing into me with glazed eyes intent on possessing every inch of me. I arched beneath him but he drove me back with the pure fury of his thrusts.

My pussy clenched as I came, tightening around him. Elijah groaned as he filled me, tipping my hips up as he drove down deeper into me.

I gasped for air as he let my legs go, draping them around his hips. "Wow," I whispered, burrowing against him.

"Yep." He held me close. "Hell, girl. I've got nothing else after that." He stroked my hair gently. "Are you okay?"

I offered him a blissed out smile. "Apart from an excess of orgasms?" I think I'm good."

"Perfect." Elijah kissed the corner of my mouth, then spent the next hour making out gently with me.

He explored, taking his time in sweet touches, but always cradling me close and never letting me go. And when I finally shifted my hips, he'd hardened inside me again. This time, he made love to me slowly, pressing our bodies together until we were both breathless. I didn't know where he started and I ended, our limbs knotting around each other as we strained and arched together. Our bodies tightened and clamped down. He filled me again and again until my thighs were sticky with his seed.

And when he left for work at the ranch, I didn't wash, needing the remnants of his brand of wild love on my skin as a mark of his possession.

I thought he'd approve. Maybe tonight I'd find out something about his life at the ranch. A part of me was nervous to discover that, but also I wanted to get to know more about him.

An hour or so after he left, my phone rang. I missed the call, but the message promised my van was ready and that someone would collect me soon.

I figured that meant I needed to get out of his bed and into my own apartment, and presentable. Lamenting the need to leave the sheets that smelled like Elijah, I made it my goal to be ready before the poor mechanic saw my walk of shame as I sneaked between the two buildings and worked out I'd been getting naughty with the baker boy next door.

Mind, in a small town like forest grove, that was probably an open secret by now, anyway.

We'd either work it out, or not. My heart gave a jerk at the thought of not having Elijah in my life. It had only been a few days, but I didn't like the idea of him not being there.

Pushing the thought aside, I dressed, gathered my favorite jacket, and headed home to grab my purse so I could pay for whatever the cost of my van would be, knowing she was about to send me broke yet again.

CHAPTER EIGHT

E LIJAH

Ash worked me hard for the hours he knew I'd be most awake for, also knowing I didn't get a huge amount of sleep the night before. I helped clear a remote road about the back of the property that had taken a bit of debris during the last heavy rainfall. No one had been out there for a while, but when one of the local girls went for a ride and came across a few fallen trees, it was time for clean up duty.

I placed the chainsaw on the ground after my third tree and shook my head at Ash. "Chain's knackered. Needs sharpening," I called over to him. "You want me to haul this lot onto the truck and head back with it? I can load it into the log pile for splitting later if you want."

Ash stretched his back and took the water I passed him. It had turned into a warm day, even though the nights were still cool. "Yeah, not a bad idea. I thought I lost you there for a while," he said soberly.

I shook my head. "You're stuck with me for a while yet, boss."

Ash winced. "Ah, I'm still not used to that. Not sure I ever will be."

"Probably a good thing. You're right to get back on your own?" I nodded to the ATV he'd brought out earlier in the day.

"Yeah. I'll be fine." He waved me away as my phone rang on the truck dash.

I reached in and picked up the device that had gotten hot where I'd left it in the sun. Damn, I needed to be more careful than that. Declan's name came up on the screen. "Sorry about the messy ship," I said cheerfully. "I did clean up, but I know we left a few things out of place—"

"Your girl's disappeared," Declan broke in.

"What?" I frowned at the phone. "I left her in the bedroom upstairs.

Declan groaned. "Did you do the dirty in my bed?"

I grimaced. "Technically, that's a shared bed," I hedged.

"You *did*. Damnit. I'm gonna leave jelly tarts in your boots, cowboy," he grunted. "Alright. Looking for...no female in my bed. And it's made." His tone lightened. "Alright, you're clear. But she's still not where she's supposed to be."

I frowned, raking my knuckles through my hair and tugging the ends. "Wait, Whaddaya mean she's not where she's supposed to be?"

"Well, the mechanic you sent her car to—"

The glitter van," I corrected.

"Yeah, that. He called earlier. said it was all done and good to go. So I went to go get her. She wasn't in the apartment, and she'd left a note on the door to the shop saying she'd gone to get the van." His voice held a heavy note, as though he was trying to tell me something.

A message that my sun-addled brain refused to process.

"Okay," I said slowly. "So maybe she's hitched a ride to go get her van?" I damn well hoped not, because we'd find out if either of us had a spanking fetish if she had.

"She left the note and was gone over an hour before the call came through on your phone that the van was ready."

"And..?" Damn, I was moving at a snail's pace today. Maybe sex was bad for my brain after all.

"Damnit, Elijah. Did you give the mechanic her number or not?"

What he was saying dawned on me. "No, I didn't." And while the Bare Bear was beautifully branded by my glitter bomb, her booking system appeared to be an online process, not an on-call one. To save her time and not interrupt when she was with clients, I assumed. But that really did beg the question... who the hell had called her and where had she gone if she thought the van was ready before it had been?

"I'm gonna call you back," I said tersely, ending the call before he could get out another word. I dialed the mechanic.

Ash sent me a hard look across the mess we'd started cleaning up. He hefted a round and tossed it onto the back of the truck. "Anything I can do to help?"

I held up a hand as the call picked up. "Hey,

have you still got the pink glitter van in there?" I listened to the man talk about how well the repairs had gone, and paid with my credit card over the phone, promising I'd come and get it later. I hung up, disquiet roiling in my stomach. Ash still watched me. I looked up at him, my throat tight. "Something's wrong."

"So go get her."

I stared at him. "I thought we just had a talk about not leaving the ranch til last."

He sent me a frown that might have bordered on an upside down grin. "If my woman is in trouble, and she causes plenty of that," he said wryly, "then I'd be out to get her as soon as I could. Go, Elijah. The ranch will wait."

I stared at him a moment longer, then my feet were moving. My truck rumbled beneath me as I backed up and headed out toward the main road, away from the ranch, leaving for the first time without wondering if I would come back or not.

Because if I didn't have Cadance, then none of it was worth anything.

"Cadance?" I called, taking the stairs to the bedroom where I'd left her asleep the night before three at a time, knowing full well that Declan had already checked and that she wasn't there. "Glitter bomb. Tell me you're hiding back here somewhere?" She wasn't, so I checked the shower, then the street.

Declan watched me with his arms folded over his apron as I paced both sides, annoying other people's customers until I reached him again. "What did she do while her van was in the shop and I wasn't here?" I didn't think Cadance was the sort of girl who would sit about doing nothing.

He grinned. "She set up shop out of a kit on the sidewalk with a folding table and called customers to her like a magnet. Damn, it was magic." Declan was one of Forest Grove's best sources of information. He listened to every rumor that came in and was excellent at telling what was utter rubbish and what consisted of true intelligence.

I scrubbed my face with my hands. "You said you were worried. Where is she?" I didn't bother keeping the begging note out of my voice.

The smile fell off his face. "You said she was a flight risk, right?"

I raised both eyebrows. "You think she's run off, left her van, her main source of income here, and somehow disappeared into the aether without anyone seeing anything today?"

That was too far a stretch for me to believe, or maybe I didn't want to believe it. I'd talked to everyone I came across and no one saw a damn thing. No mechanic came down the street, no one saw her get into a car, truck or onto a bike and drive away. No buses came through town today, so it wasn't that either. No one had seen her at all.

Declan's eyes darkened. "You think it's the ex?"

I'd told him about the knife incident when I explained what I was using my half of my savings for, rather than investing it into the business for the quarter. Declan thought I was crazy, but seemed to understand, at least since she kept coming round even though I didn't think they'd met yet.

"Yeah, I think he might have tracked her." I matched his expression. "Not that the soft man she described seemed like a tracker. But still, obsession drives a man."

Declan nodded. "Where would he take her?"

I closed my eyes. "Home? Out of state? Fuck, anywhere." Desperation brewed in my gut as I paced the sidewalk again.

"Have you called the police?"

I shot him a look. "She's been missing for a few hours at most. You know they'll say to wait."

He acknowledged that with a nod. "Alright, so when's the last time you saw her?"

I ran through the exercise with him, grateful he drew my panic back from the edge of pure self destruction. I leaned my head back against the wall of her building. "I know nothing about her. I've had days to learn something about her past and I never. Fucking. Asked." I punctuated every word with a rap of the side of my fist against the brickwork. My last hit her door. That creaked open.

I glanced at it, then at Declan. He held my gaze. "Have you checked—"

I shook my head. "No. Did you?"

"Get up there, sunshine."

Her staircase was a whole lot narrower and dimmer than mine, with a light out near the top in a high stairwell. This part of the building was older than ours, while the one that Declan and I shared had been renovated when we decided to do up the bakery. But the side that Cadance rented hadn't been upgraded for a long time and was well overdue.

I reached the door at the top of the stairs, her name on my lips, when a voice reached me. A thin, nasally voice that didn't match my girl.

A man's voice.

"—strutting around town in a dress anyone can see through. Look, you're not even wearing a bra, like a common whore. No wonder he was all over you so fast with your teats tumbling out like a used up cow's."

My blood went from regular temperature to boiling in less than half a second. This had to be the ex husband. Not only had she suffered physical abuse at his hand, but this bullshit too. I gritted my teeth, my hands already on the door, prepared to bust it open, but the asshole wasn't close to done.

"Look at you, his jizz all over you, staining you up. Is that what you've become, Charity? A slut who will open her legs to anyone? I watched you last night. Both of you." My stomach plummeted as he jeered at her. *This is my fault.* Dammit, I should have turned off the lights, taken her somewhere else. "Watched him like anyone else could have, front row to a live porn show starring my own fucking *wife.*"

"I'm not your wife," Candance spat out. Scuffling noises happened behind the door as I slammed my shoulder into it. Her name jammed in my throat. "I haven't been that for a long time, Bradley." A hand cracked across skin on the other side of the door. Cadance whimpered and fell quiet.

Her name ripped from my lips as I slammed my body weight against the wood. Something splintered and I stumbled through a gap that hadn't been there before, mostly the right size for me. I kicked shards out of the way and advanced on a man who I swore shouldn't have been half the size he was. But part of me was okay with the fact he stood at my height. Because now I had no problem with unleashing every inch of the pent up fury I had in me for everything this man had done to hurt the woman who cowered on the floor at his feet.

My stunning glitter bomb. The woman with defiance in her eyes and a flirtatious smile on her lips. Who lived loud and proud and free.

Who should never kneel for a man when she didn't choose that course of action, and sure as hell not outside playtime together.

My fist cracked into the son of a bitch's face. He stumbled back, something akin to shock or bemusement written there before the pain set in. I wondered if he'd ever discovered true pain before. If not, jail was gonna be one hell of a trip for him. I hoped he enjoyed it for a real long time.

Voices shouted beyond me, and I knelt to crouch over Cadance as police, tailed by Declan who I knew wouldn't want to miss the action at all, swarmed the small apartment who barely fit us, let alone six other men.

My girl trembled in my arms as I cradled her close to my chest, tucked into my body. "Glitter bomb. Are you able to tell me if he hurt you? Do I need to get you a paramedic?" I kissed her temple as feet rushed around us and the asshole was dragged away.

She shivered in my arms. "He just slapped me a few times."

Declan crouched beside me. "Hey, beauty girl. I have a space beside a hot oven if you want. There's also wine in the fridge, and treats. Not that I'm feeding addictions." He held up his hands in defence at my look. "Just trying to help."

She hiccuped as the first tears I'd ever seen her shed tumbled down her cheeks. "Thanks, Declan." My gaze slid across to her. "What?" She shrugged. "I told you I researched my neighbors. He's the nosy one. You were the pretty gourd boy."

"Is that right?" I planted my ass on her carpet and pulled her into the circle of my legs. "I think the police are gonna wanna talk to you. Wanna do that in the shop or up here?"

"Here," she said immediately as I raised an eyebrow. "Then shop with treats?" she asked hopefully. Her mood dropped. "Then I have to go pay for my van."

I kissed the top of her head. "Gotcha covered, glitter bomb." Her head snapped up, and she winced. "What did you do, Elijah?"

Declan edged out of the room as I laughed and dipped my head to cover her mouth with mine before she could protest again. We were still kissing indecently on her floor when the first police officer arrived to take her statement.

EPILOGUE

CADANCE

Elijah's cabin was the perfect size for us. All my fears of not fitting in at the ranch were cast aside the moment I stepped into the found family community who adopted me just as they had adopted Elijah and everyone else who came along. Just like they adopted new rescues. I figured I was one of those, and so I suited the theme.

I still wasn't sure who was healing who out of Elijah and me, or if it matters. Right now, we were happy working side by side at the ranch, and spending evenings together. I still wasn't sure how I felt about him blindsiding me on paying for my van repairs, but that was three months back and he'd made me a stack of pretty treats to make up for it. Somehow that seemed butt about, but he kept trying and his creatures grew more and more creative...so really, who was I to complain?

"What's this one?" I traced the patterns on the back of what I thought was a turtle shell, but because I knew it would also end up in a matching gourd that would complete the art work, and give perspective to the piece, I had stopped guessing months back.

"Green sea turtle. I know it's a bit out of the ordinary, but Declan organized our first tour bus and got us on a few tourist websites, so now we're an official destination.

I squealed and looped my arms around his neck, pressing my lips to his. "That's incredible," I breathed. "Do you want socials done? Get him to send me everything," I demanded.

Declan had happily handed me their socials accounts and interactive newsletter that Elijah didn't even know existed. I'd resurrected the poor thing and it had increased foot traffic from other local towns too. Now, weekends were big trade days and we spent more time during the week fulfilling preorders for coming events and weekends than anything else.

"I'm so excited for you," I glowed at him.

"Mmhm." He fidgeted and I stopped.

As in, everything stopped.

"What?" he asked warily.

"That." I pointed to his twisting fingers.

He quickly hid them. "It's nothing."

"Spill," I demanded.

Because my boy never fidgeted for no reason. Even when he thought he did, he didn't. Unless he was trying to keep a secret. Elijah Campise really sucked at those.

He dipped his head and kissed me, the sort of long, slow kiss that said we'd be here for a while. The sort that stole my breath as he pushed me back against the wall and slid his knee between mine.

A moan built low in my chest. I broke away, gasping and shoved at his shoulders. "That was a naughty distraction technique," I betrayed him, slapping his chest lightly.

"Was it." Large hands squeezed my waist, leaving need zinging through me.

"Very," I murmured, all too aware of my breasts suddenly heavy beneath my t-shirt, without any bra. One hand crept up to squeeze gently, milking my nipple. I swore my eyes rolled back in my head. "Stop that," I moaned as he levered his knee higher.

"Stop what?" Elijah teased, dipping his head to brush his mouth over mine. "Stop making you come in that short little denim skirt? You know better than to wear something like that around me." He pushed his knee higher and I opened my eyes when he growled. "Glitter bomb..."

"What?" I said innocently.

The hand grasping my breast dropped to slide between my legs. I moaned as he speared two fingers straight inside me. "No. Fucking. Panties."

"Oh. That," I said faintly, bearing down on his hand.

"Ride me," he instructed, working gently, but leaving the greater work to me. I did as he demanded, driving my hips downward, chasing the pleasure that was just out of reach. My core tightened. I leaned forward—

Elijah's mouth crushed mine as he pushed me back, pumping his hand into me. I screamed into his mouth, coming too fast. Something caught my wrist tight for a moment before he released me, then my orgasms ripped into me. My legs shook, and I collapsed against his chest, little more than a soaked, trembling mess.

Elijah pressed his wet fingers to my lips, coating them. I sucked them clean then offered him my mouth. He kissed me greedily like I knew he would, savoring the taste of me before he dropped to his knees, pushing me back to the wall. I closed my eyes, floating as he took me through another orgasm.

I rocked my hips gently over his face, leaning my weight safely on him, the ultimate trust exercise between us. I came on a soft cry and he gathered me into his arms, carrying me to the sofa where we both collapsed in a tangle of limbs.

"That was...Wow." I closed my eyes and sank into his embrace, listening to his heart beat fast against my cheek.

"Mm. Wear this skirt more often for me, glitter bomb?" He ran his fingers along my arm, down to my wrist and back again.

I remembered the pressure on my wrist and glanced down, expecting to see a cheap pair of sex shop handcuffs dangling from them. But around my wrist, in perfect miniature, was a bracelet of tiny, carved gourds. And between each was a glittery, pink bead.

I marveled at the workmanship of each carving, as always stunned at his work, how much time and care he took with each one.

"When did you do this?" I turned the bracelet around, unable to pick a favorite. Each was as delicate as the next, and each was individual. It must have taken him hours.

He shrugged. "You know if I don't sleep a lot, even though I have you. So, I wanted to make you something. It's not an engagement ring, not yet. I figured you'd been tied to the wrong man before, and that you wouldn't want to rush." He tipped my chin back so I could see his eyes, the question there in them. He'd never asked me about my real name, and he'd never forced me to go back to it. I settled in to listen. "And I don't want to rush you, Cadance. But I wanted to make something. I wanted to give you something that came from me." His voice thickened on that last, and my sight blurred.

"It's beautiful. Thank you," I whispered, over-whelmed. "And it's perfect for us." I snuggled into him.

He was right. I didn't need an engagement ring, and I didn't need a white wedding. I'd had both of those things before and look how that had turned out. Elijah gave me the sort of fairytale love I'd always dreamed about. Selfless, fun, with a solid dose of flirtation and friendship underneath. That's who we were. And his gift was so beautiful, beyond anything I could manage.

I giggled. "I mean, I can give you a pedicure? I don't know what I can give you in return," I said wistfully.

He laughed and stretched. "You can paint me whatever color you like, glitter girl. And you give me plenty every day."

I smiled, sinking into the shape of him. Maybe, if he was lucky, I'd find some of that powdered sugar, or that strawberry sticky jam stuff he seemed to keep in excess and we could make one hell of a sticky mess together. Something to make my gourd boy good enough to eat.

Thank you so much for reading Elijah and Cadance's too gourd to be true story (the puns just won't stop. I'm not sorry). Please do leave a review. They really do feed authors, and we exist on coffee. Want to read more about the ranch that Elijah used to work at?
Start reading Red Hart Ranch HERE.

ALPHAS FALL HARD

Available now: Dive into the Alphas Fall Hard Collection. Each standalone novel introduces a brooding hero and the strong woman who turns his world upside down. From cozy cabins to bustling pumpkin patches, experience the magic of love blossoming amidst the hues of autumn, set on the Off-Duty Rescue Ranch in Montana.

READ THE SERIES HERE

Cozy Cabin for Two - Zee Irwin

His Little Pumpkin - Haley Travis

Falling for the Lumbersnack - Lyssa J. Cole

Autumn Be His Wife - Nyla Lily

Gourd Enough to Eat - Sofia Aves

Harvest His Heart - Engrid Eaves

Frosty in Flannel - Patricia Mason and Joann Baker

ABOUT THE AUTHOR

USA *Today* Bestselling author Sofia Aves writes fast-paced police romances, sizzling military units, steamy cowboys with a Montana backdrop and the occasional cheeky god. Sofia writes kidlit for charity and has over one hundred and fifty publications across five not-so-super-secret pen names. As acquisitions editor for Evernight and Evernight Teen publishing she loves discovering new talent in romance and YA spaces, and is a mum of three crazies in a returned veteran household. Sofia has two overly large fur babies who think they're teacup puppies, a duck who prefers to eat from a dog bowl and two axolotls named after a dragon and a firebird.

Sofia lives near Brisbane, Australia, where she has her own alpaca park, Lorendel.

www.sofiaaves.com

Sign up to <u>Sofia's newsletter</u> and get a free Blue Blooded Brothers book.

Haven't read the Z Boy's prequel? Get it for free here:
A TABLE FOR TEN
Follow Sofia on
BookBub
Twitter
Instagram

READ SOFIA'S SERIES

Blue Blooded Brothers
Collision
Politics & Paperwork
Blindsided
Sentinel
Mugshots & Candy Canes
Impact
Reckoning
Red Hart Ranch
Snow on the Range
Siren on the Range
Sundown on the Range
Spirit on the Range
Ash on the Range
Mistletoe on the Range (2025)

Forgotten Mountain Man

Texan Devils

Ranger's Wish

Ranger Bedevilled

Ranger's Passion

Ranger's Fury

Ranger's Wrath

Ranger's Storm

Snapdragons & Seductions

Summer with a Ranger

Merry with a Ranger

Beach Duty Collection

Playing to Win

Off Boarding

Vicious Slash

Zero Pointer

Off Stage Fling

Rippton Allstars

Crushing It

Glacial Force

Rippton Creatives

Study Games

Make Me, Break Me

Twisted Obsession

Spring Break with a Mafia Prince

A Royally Fake French Menage

Angel Shot

Jericho Chimeras

Puck Me Always

Puck My Heart

Puck me Sideways

Z Boys

King

Joker

Hearts

Ace

Mayhem & Mistletoe

Ruski

Fast Track to Love

Speed Trap

Klauss Brothers

Zander

Keegan

Gallo Empire *with Jade Marshall*

Splintered Vows

Fractured Vows

Fierce Vows

Savage Covenant

Rom Coms

She's A Hot Christmas Mess

Boats, Moats and Root Beer Floats

Writing Romantasy as
SOFIA SHELLEY
Dead Poets Sorority

Writing Reverse Harem Dark Romance as
DOVE PRIEST
Recurve Ridge

Kidlit writing as
JO SEYSENER
The OCD Elf
The OCD Elf's Great Reindeer Calamity
Greg and the Egg

writing YA as
JOSS PHOENIX
Alchem Academy
HIDE FROM US

. . .

Writing spicy paranormal romance as

RAVEN HUSH

Club Fray

Darkest Desires

Purge

Kidnapped By Claws

Ruin

Shadow Lords

Sinner's End

Heaven's Gate (2026)

Monster Brides

Phoenix's Eternal Flame

Kraken's Vow

Krampus' Christmas Bride

Silent Sentinels Duet

Reflections of Silence

Echoes in the Void

Monsters In New York

Feral Moon Rising

Dark Water Refuge

www.ingramcontent.com/pod-product-compliance
Lightning Source LLC
Chambersburg PA
CBHW052016170626
46808CB00007B/2950